PUPPY

To

Zane

"Dare to Dream"

William B. Stringer, Sr.

William B. Stringer, Sr.

ISBN 978-1-64140-222-4 (paperback)
ISBN 978-1-64191-996-8 (hardcover)
ISBN 978-1-64140-223-1 (digital)

Christian Faith Publishing, Inc.
832 Park Avenue
Meadville, PA 16335
www.christianfaithpublishing.com

Printed in the United States of America

1

Let me share a very interesting story about a puppy whose life was much like the life of so many people and animals on this planet that we live on. This is a story about Puppy's life.

Puppy is a little, bitty dog—not just a little, bitty dog but a very, small, baby dog—a dog much smaller than any other newborn baby dog. To say it another way, Puppy was a runt. A runt is a dog that is born much smaller than any other newly born puppy dog.

But Puppy's mommy and daddy dogs loved Puppy just as much as they loved Puppy's brothers and sisters in the dog family. As a matter of fact, Mommy and Daddy Dog loved Puppy so much that they gave even more

attention to Puppy because Puppy needed to know that Puppy was loved just as much as the other dogs in the family.

Mommy Dog and Daddy Dog and Puppy's brother and sister dogs were all being raised in their human owners' house. They were fed regularly. They were kept clean every day, and they had a nice, warm doggy bed to sleep in at night.

Puppy's dog family did not have to worry about anything. Everything was just right. There was no need to worry about how they would be treated by anyone or anything inside—or outside—of Puppy's home.

Puppy felt safe as Puppy snuggled up against Puppy's mommy dog or daddy dog. Puppy never feared anything or anyone, because Puppy knew that Puppy's mommy dog and daddy dog were always close by to protect Puppy.

As Puppy began to grow, Puppy began to explore the home that Puppy lived in. Puppy would go from one room to another, to see what new things Puppy could see. Sometimes, Puppy would see light coming from a place that was a bit higher than Puppy could reach. Puppy began to wonder what that light was and where it came from.

Puppy would ask Mommy Dog and Daddy Dog what that light was and "where did that light come from."

Mommy Dog and Daddy Dog explained that the light Puppy saw during the day time was coming from what was called a window and the sun—at least that is what humans called it.

Puppy hoped that, someday, Puppy would be able to grow a bit more so that Puppy could look out of that window thing and see where the light stuff was coming from, and see what was on the other side of that window thing.

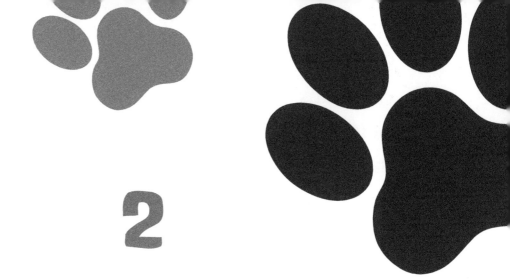

2

As Puppy continued to grow and Puppy's brother and sister dogs began to get new owners, Puppy felt a bit lonely without Puppy's sister and brother dogs to play with and run around the yard with.

Puppy also found out that Puppy was not able to get a new owner like Puppy's brother and sister dogs. Puppy could not understand why. But Puppy did know one thing. Puppy knew that Puppy's mommy and daddy dog still loved Puppy very much.

Puppy also knew that Mommy and Daddy dog did not always have control over Puppy's life like Puppy wished they could have. After all, Puppy was owned by Puppy's human owner.

Humans were okay, but sometimes humans made decisions or choices that even humans didn't want to make. But decisions had to be made! So, one day, Puppy's human owners made the decision to put Puppy outside in their big backyard.

At first Puppy was excited about living in the backyard in a new dog house. Puppy could run around in the yard and chase butterflies and bumblebees. Puppy could see that sun thing every day and look at that window thing from outside.

Puppy was able to understand and see things that Puppy had never seen before. This part of Puppy's new life was so exciting and new. Puppy was in dog heaven.

3

Puppy did not know anything about the summer, winter, spring, or fall seasons. Puppy did not know the time of the year or the season in which Puppy was placed in the backyard to live.

Puppy just knew that the sun thing was nice and warm, and that Puppy enjoyed the light that it gave.

But still, Puppy was growing even bigger in size, and that fence thing that was all around the backyard was beginning to look smaller and smaller.

So, one day, Puppy's human owners had to make another decision—decision that Puppy was not too happy about. Puppy's human owners had to put a collar around Puppy's neck and tie Puppy to a tree close to the dog house.

Puppy did not like that very much because Puppy could no longer run around the yard like Puppy liked to do. Puppy could only go so far.

Often, Puppy would pull a little on the rope that was tied to the tree to see if it would stretch or maybe even pull loose from the tree. But it did not stretch or pull loose.

Puppy also noticed something else. Puppy noticed that the nights were beginning to get a little bit cooler and Puppy had to get closer to the straw that was in the dog house.

Well, as time went on, the days and nights began to get cooler and cooler. And then the days began to get cold! Puppy did not like the cold days and the cold nights.

Puppy did not like being tied to that old tree. Puppy did not like being cold and not able to run around and get warm. Puppy was becoming angry.

So Puppy began to pull harder and harder on that old rope that was tied around that big, old tree.

4

Puppy wanted to run around and get warm. Puppy wanted to be free to move around and see new things and to see Mommy and Daddy Dog again. Puppy wanted to have a new human owner that had room for Puppy.

Every day, Puppy pulled on that old rope. Puppy tugged on that old rope that was tied around that big, old tree. Puppy wanted to be free.

One day, Puppy pulled and pulled on that old rope and, to Puppy's surprise, that old rope broke and Puppy ran and jumped over that small fence that Puppy had grown bigger than.

Puppy knew that Puppy would miss Puppy's mommy and daddy dog, but Puppy had to find a new home. After all, Puppy was now a grown dog and Puppy needed to be the big dog that Mommy and Daddy Dog had told Puppy that Puppy would one day become.

As Puppy ran and ran, Puppy got farther and farther from where Puppy had lived for four years. Puppy remembered the good old days with Mommy and Daddy Dog. Puppy remembered how Puppy had played with Puppy's sister and brother dogs. Puppy's sister and brother dogs had been placed with a new owner and were probably very happy in their new homes.

Puppy wanted a new home and a new owner to love, and to be cared for like any good dog would. Puppy was hungry and Puppy had to find some food to eat and water to drink. Puppy would walk through alleys to look for food, and look for streams to drink water from.

Puppy was lonely but was reminded that Puppy was now a big dog and that Puppy had to find Puppy's way in the world.

One day, Puppy was eating a hamburger that someone had dropped on the ground and as Puppy looked up and around, Puppy saw a bunch of other dogs following each other around. There was something strange in the air and Puppy began to follow the other dogs.

5

As Puppy followed the other dogs, Puppy did not notice that Puppy was being followed by a human with a big, old net. Puppy's attention was on those other dogs. Puppy was following them to see what was in the air that seemed strange.

As Puppy followed far behind the other dogs, Puppy still did not realize that Puppy was being followed by that strange human with a big, old net.

And just as Puppy was about to catch up with the other dogs, Puppy was caught by that big, old net that was in the human person's hands. Puppy tried to tug and pull away from that old net but was not able to get away.

The human with the net was as gentle as possible, but the human had to catch Puppy because that was the human's job. The human was a dog catcher and the human's job was to catch and save dogs from being killed in traffic, or going hungry and starving to death.

But Puppy did not know this. Puppy was afraid and did not know what the human wanted to do with Puppy. So Puppy finally gave up because Puppy had become tired trying to get away.

Puppy was put in a big truck thing and placed in a cage. Puppy did not know what a truck or cage was. Puppy only knew that it was all new to Puppy and Puppy was not very happy. Puppy was not happy because Puppy did not know what was to become of Puppy and where Puppy was now going.

The truck thing began to move and bump around the streets that the truck thing rode on. It seemed to go on and on until, finally, the truck thing stopped!

Puppy's cage thing was removed from the truck thing and moved to a large room that had larger cage things where other dogs were placed.

Puppy was afraid but Puppy noticed that the other dogs in the other large, cage things all had smiles on their dog faces. Puppy also noticed that the other dogs did not seem hungry, and they also looked nice and clean.

6

Puppy remembered that when Puppy lived on the streets, Puppy had to beg or even fight other dogs for food. But these other dogs in the big cages seemed eager to share the food that was in the big cage things.

Puppy could not believe Puppy's eyes. Someone did seem to care about other dogs, and someone was willing to take Puppy in and care for Puppy. But Puppy wanted a home of Puppy's own.

A kind and gentle-speaking human reached out to Puppy who was now in one of those big cage things. The kind human reached out very carefully to touch Puppy and then pet Puppy.

Puppy could see that this kind, gentle human was a friend and wanted to be a friend to Puppy. So Puppy let the kind, gentle human pet Puppy.

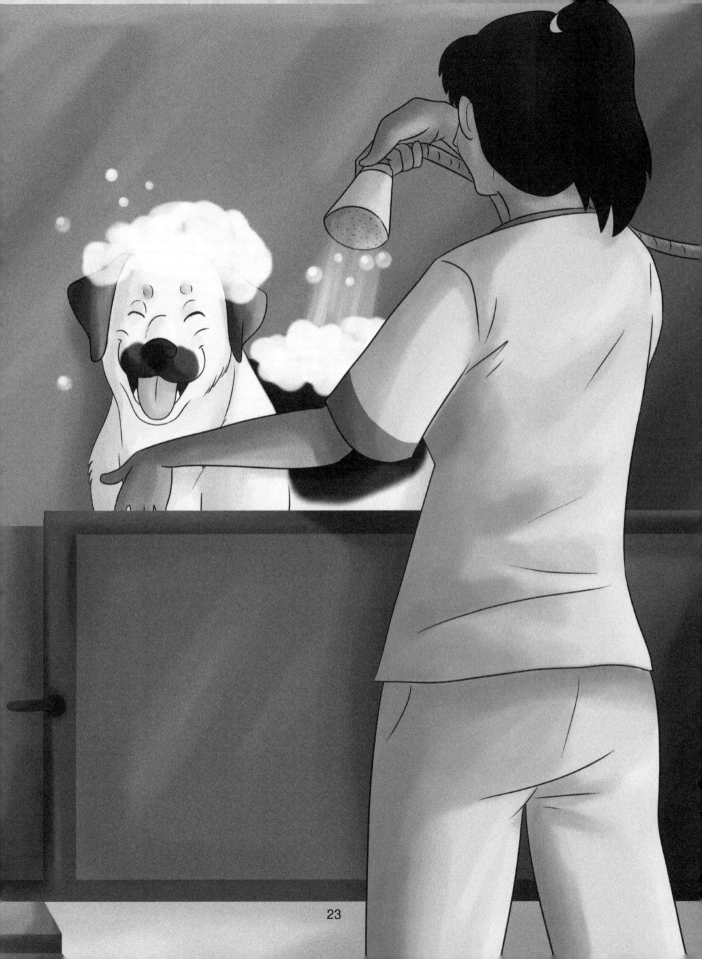

After it was over, the kind, gentle human was able to take Puppy and give Puppy a nice, soapy bath. Puppy liked this and was very happy to be clean again. Puppy was excited and wagged Puppy's tail, and licked the hand of this kind, gentle human.

Now Puppy could eat the big meal that was placed in that big cage thing that no longer seemed to be so bad. "Not bad at all," Puppy said.

As each day went by, Puppy began to think about Puppy's dog family. Puppy remembered all the lessons that Mommy and Daddy Dog had taught Puppy.

Puppy was told by Mommy and Daddy Dog that Puppy too would have a new owner who would treat Puppy as a favored pet.

Puppy was not quite content about that, but Puppy was happy for what Puppy now had. Puppy remembered the times with Puppy's sister and brother dogs, and when Puppy had seen them leave home one by one to be with new owners.

Puppy wanted to have a new owner also. But Puppy was okay where Puppy was for now.

7

One day, Puppy was enjoying playing with a ball thing called a toy. Puppy was running around in the big cage thing, chasing the ball thing, not noticing someone strangely looking at Puppy as Puppy continued to play with Puppy's ball thing.

Puppy heard a strange clanging at the door thing of that big, old cage thing. As Puppy looked around to see what that strange noise was Puppy noticed that cage door thing was open.

A tall strange human went over to Puppy and reached gently toward Puppy. Puppy watched and the human carefully reached out to Puppy to see if Puppy would bite.

Puppy had already experienced the kindness of the other humans and trusted that the other humans would not let this new human hurt Puppy. So, Puppy let the strange, new human pet Puppy. Puppy licked the stranger's hand and immediately the stranger drew Puppy close and hugged Puppy as Puppy had ever been hugged before!

There was something different about this human. There was a different touch and a different smell about this human. This human had a way of making Puppy feel safe and loved!

Puppy knew that this human was special. Puppy somehow felt that Mommy and Daddy Dog had told Puppy right—that one day someone special would come into Puppy's life. Puppy would be found by someone who would take Puppy closer to them than Puppy had ever been.

The stranger took Puppy in the stranger's arms, carried Puppy outside of that big, old cage thing and took Puppy to that stranger's home. But this human was no longer a stranger for this human took Puppy in and cared for Puppy as Puppy had never been cared for before.

As Puppy laid in Puppy's soft, warm bed—after Puppy had eaten a warm meal and drank fresh water—Puppy was reminded of that if Puppy ever had a chance to help another lost, lonely dog, Puppy would share everything that Puppy had with that dog.

For Puppy was lost and now found, safe, and no longer hungry. Puppy had a home, a loving human master and the chance to learn that Puppy should never give up, no matter what!

About the Author

William B. Stringer, Sr. is the father of two sons who he enjoyed telling stories to when they were toddlers. He is currently pastoring a church in Dayton, Ohio. Bill originally wrote the story of "Puppy" to include it with his first sermon in 1989 as a licensed preacher. His passion is in letting young men and women know that they can overcome any negative experiences that have been a part of their early development.

CPSIA information can be obtained
at www.ICGtesting.com
Printed in the USA
BVHW02*1219150918
527585BV00006B/11/P

9 781641 919968